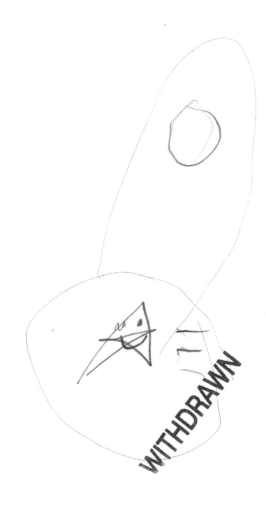

Dear Parent:

Congratulations! Your child is taking the first steps on an exciting journey. The destination? Independent reading!

STEP INTO READING® will help your child get there. The program offers five steps to reading success. Each step includes fun stories and colorful art. There are also Step into Reading Sticker Books, Step into Reading Math Readers, Step into Reading Write-In Readers, Step into Reading Phonics Readers, and Step into Reading Phonics First Steps! Boxed Sets—a complete literacy program with something for every child.

Learning to Read, Step by Step!

Ready to Read   Preschool–Kindergarten
• big type and easy words • rhyme and rhythm • picture clues
For children who know the alphabet and are eager to begin reading.

Reading with Help   Preschool–Grade 1
• basic vocabulary • short sentences • simple stories
For children who recognize familiar words and sound out new words with help.

Reading on Your Own   Grades 1–3
• engaging characters • easy-to-follow plots • popular topics
For children who are ready to read on their own.

Reading Paragraphs   Grades 2–3
• challenging vocabulary • short paragraphs • exciting stories
For newly independent readers who read simple sentences with confidence.

Ready for Chapters   Grades 2–4
• chapters • longer paragraphs • full-color art
For children who want to take the plunge into chapter books but still like colorful pictures.

STEP INTO READING® is designed to give every child a successful reading experience. The grade levels are only guides. Children can progress through the steps at their own speed, developing confidence in their reading, no matter what their grade.

Remember, a lifetime love of reading starts with a single step!

For my princess, Ramona

Copyright © 2006 Disney Enterprises, Inc. All rights reserved. Published in the United States by Random House Children's Books, a division of Random House, Inc., New York, in conjunction with Disney Enterprises, Inc.
www.stepintoreading.com
www.randomhouse.com/kids/disney
Educators and librarians, for a variety of teaching tools, visit us at
www.randomhouse.com/teachers
Library of Congress Cataloging-in-Publication Data
Jordan, Apple.
    Winter wishes.
        p. cm. — (Step into reading. Step 2 book)
Summary: Disney princesses from Snow White to Cinderella enjoy indoor and outdoor wintertime activities, from baking cookies and drinking hot cocoa to riding through the snow in a sleigh.
ISBN-13: 978-0-7364-2409-7 (trade)
ISBN-10: 0-7364-2409-1 (trade)
ISBN-13: 978-0-7364-8049-9 (lib. bdg.)
ISBN-10: 0-7364-8049-8 (lib. bdg.)
[1. Winter—Fiction. 2. Princesses—Fiction. 3. Stories in rhyme.] I. Title. II. Series.
PZ8.3.J7645Wi 2006   [E]—dc22   2005028915

Printed in the United States of America 21 20 19 18 17   First Edition
STEP INTO READING, RANDOM HOUSE, and the Random House colophon are registered trademarks of Random House, Inc.

STEP INTO READING®

STEP 2

DISNEY
◆ PRINCESS

Winter Wishes

by Apple Jordan
illustrated by Elisa Marrucchi

Random House 🏠 New York

Winter is here!

Chilly winds blow.

The outside sparkles.

There is so much snow.

It is a frosty season.

There is a lot to do.

It is the time of year
when wishes come true.

Outside is coated
with fluffy snow.
Inside, Snow White
pours cups of cocoa.

She trims the tree
with stars and bells.

She fills the cottage
with warm cookie smells.

She makes a wish
on a star so bright.

Then the Dwarfs sing and dance into the night.

Ariel wishes
for a wintry bash.

A holiday parade
makes a big splash!

The jolly friends
dance around the tree.
Winter is fun
under the sea.

Lovely Belle wishes
for a big winter feast.
Mrs. Potts makes one
for her and the Beast.

The meal is served
and piled up high.
Roast turkey, cider,
and warm apple pie!

Everyone shares
in the holiday cheer.

It is such a joy
to have friends so dear.

Briar Rose sings
a wishful love song.
A snowbird sweetly
chirps right along.

Sing, strum,
hum, tweet!
A winter concert
never sounded
so sweet.

Jasmine wishes to see

a world with snow . . .

. . . and a snowman
dressed in a hat
and a bow!

Abracadabra!
Alakazoo!
Genie makes her
wish come true.

26

Cinderella wishes to go
on a snowy coach ride.
So Prince Charming
takes his lovely bride.

The coach brings them
to a grand winter ball.

Then they happily dance
in the snowfall.

Make a winter wish.

It is fun to do.

You never know when

the dream may come true.